*To Véronique
and Didier*

Translated by Daniel Geluyckens

Production © 1993 Rainbow Grafics Intl-Baronian Books. All rights
reserved. Printed in Belgium. No part of this book may be reproduced
or copied in any form without written permission from the publisher.
All trademarks are the property of Western Publishing Company, Inc.,
Racine, Wisconsin 53404. ISBN: 0-307-17502-2   A MCMXCIII

Library of Congress Cataloging-in-Publication Data
Rosy.
Basil / Rosy.
p.   cm.
Summary: Pondering the fact that his dog Basil plays while he works, a boy decides that
if they work together Basil could go on to become a teacher, astronaut, or president.
$13.95
[1. Dogs—fiction.] I Title.
PZ7.R7238Bas 1993

[E]—dc20   92-46053
                                                                             CIP
                                                                             AC

BASIL

BY ROSY

ARTISTS & WRITERS GUILD ™

GOLDEN BOOKS
WESTERN PUBLISHING COMPANY, INC.
850 THIRD AVENUE, NEW YORK, NEW YORK 10022

I have a dog.
His name is BASIL.

It isn't fair!
When I work, he plays.

In the evening,
I do my homework.
He watches TV with my dad.

Surely,
   we could work together.

During recess,
we would be the best.

On winter vacation,
we would be champs.

At the end of the school year, he could get a diploma.

And later,
he could be,
let us say,
a doctor.

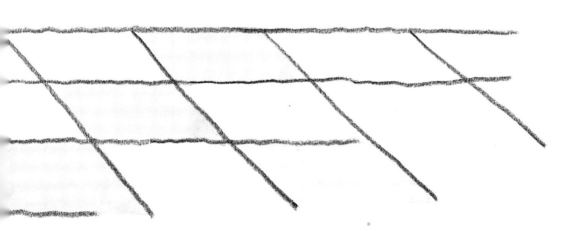

Or an astronaut.

Or perhaps,
the President of the United States.

Or even,
a teacher!

And when he was working,
I could play!